Richard Scarry's
Planes and Rockets and Things That Fly

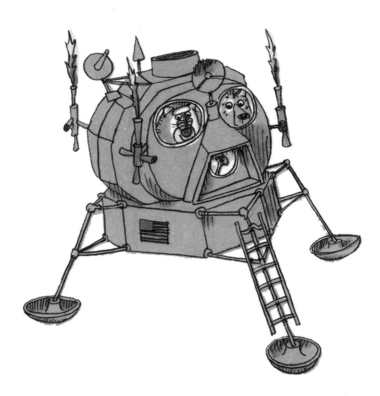

These stories first published in Great Britain in Great Big Air Book in 1971, except for Grandma
Cat Comes to Visit, first published in Great Britain in Busiest People Ever in 1976.

This collection published by HarperCollins Children's Books in 2011.
HarperCollins Children's Books is a division of HarperCollins Publishers Ltd,
77-85 Fulham Palace Road, London W6 8JB

1 3 5 7 9 10 8 6 4 2

ISBN: 978-0-00-743286-8

© 2011, 1976, 1971 Richard Scarry Corporation.

The HarperCollins website address is www.harpercollins.co.uk

Printed and bound in China.

Richard Scarry's
Planes and Rockets and Things That Fly

HarperCollins *Children's Books*

How Aeroplanes Fly

Father Cat took Huckle and Little Sister to the airport to meet Rudolf, the famous pilot. He was going to show them how to fly an aeroplane.

First, Rudolf pointed to the cockpit. "The pilot sits here," he said. "He flies the aeroplane with the stick, the throttle and the pedals. The stick is used to move the elevators on the rear wings up and down. They help the plane to fly lower or higher.

"The stick also moves the ailerons on the front wings up and down. These help to make the plane tip sideways and turn. The pedals move the rudder on the tail. This helps the plane to turn smoothly.

control tower

Rudder

Tail

Elevator

Cockpit

Propeller

Fuselage

Nose

Aileron

Wing

Landing gear

A mechanic fixing a motor

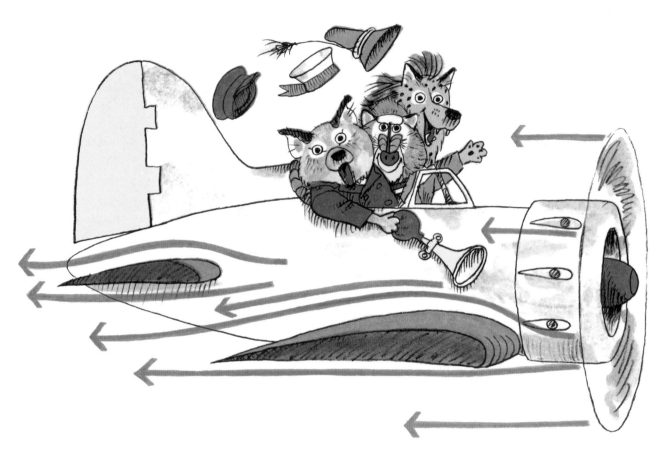

"The spinning propeller pulls the plane forward, and makes the air slip around the wing.
The air that goes over the curved top of the wing moves fast. But along
the straight bottom of the wing the air moves slower.
This makes it push harder, and it lifts the plane up, up into the sky."

"One day I'll fly an aeroplane," said Huckle.
"Yes, maybe," said Rudolf. "But for now
come flying with me."

Huckle Takes Flying Lessons

"First, everyone fasten his seatbelt," said Rudolf.
"I will start the engine and set the propeller to spinning.
Down the runway we speed. Faster! Faster!"

A Fall Through the Air

"With the stick, I can also make the plane tip
sideways by moving the ailerons on the wings
like this… The plane leans over sideways.

"I push the stick forward.
The elevators are pulled down.
This forces the nose of the plane down.

"I pull back on the stick
and level out.

"I'll pull back on the stick. The elevators are pulled up.
The moving air strikes them and pushes the tail down. This, together with the
pressure under the wings, forces the nose up. I fold up the landing gear and push
the stick forward a little bit. Now we are flying level."

"Then I turn over. I…!

"Now I climb steeply.

"Oh! Oh! I've fallen out!
I forgot to fasten my seat belt!

"But I, Rudolf Strudel, am lucky!
I never fail to wear my parachute.
The air is trapped in the parachute letting me
fall slowly to earth. But I wonder if Huckle will
be able to land the plane safely all by himself."

Huckle Lands the Plane

Huckle quickly grabbed the control stick and located the pedals.

By working the rudder, the ailerons and the elevators just as Rudolf had shown him, he started to come down to land.

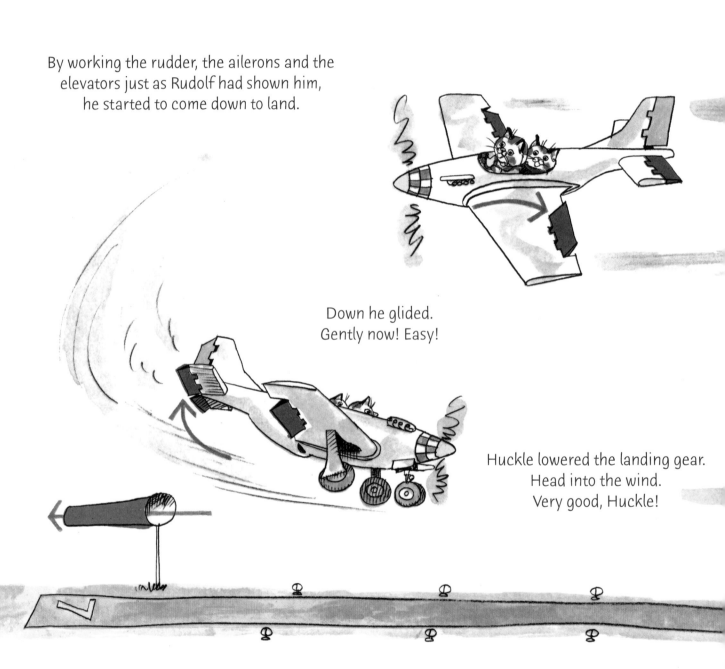

Down he glided.
Gently now! Easy!

Huckle lowered the landing gear.
Head into the wind.
Very good, Huckle!

Touchdown! A perfect landing.
You are an excellent pilot, Huckle.

...And another perfect landing.
Right in the pickle barrel!
Very good, Rudolf.

PICKLES

How Birds Fly

Birds can fly in the air.
Just watch Charlie Crow.
First, his legs push him into the air.

Then his wings open. They move upward and forward as he pulls his legs close to his body.

Then Charlie flaps his wings downward and to the rear.
His feathers close tightly together again. The downward
beat of his wings moves him forward in the air.
He uses his tail feathers to steer.
Now Charlie spreads his wings to slow down.
He is ready to land.

Oh, dear! He's stopped too fast!
He's a good flier, but he doesn't
always land so well.

Harry Hyena thinks that if he glues feathers on
his arms and tail – and then flaps his arms –
he will be able to fly like a bird.
Well, he is wrong.

A Summer Picnic

It was a bright, sunny summer day. There was not a cloud in the sky.
Miss Honey and her boyfriend, Bruno, decided to take all the children on a picnic.

They drove past a lake where
some fishermen were fishing.
Oh, oh! They seem to have caught something!

While they were setting out the picnic, Rudolf Strudel,
the famous aeroplane pilot, dropped by.
"Miss Honey!" he said. "A big thunderstorm is coming this way!
You and the children must take shelter immediately!"

Ants always
come to picnics!

Everyone had been too busy putting out food to
notice the black storm clouds gathering in the sky.
"Hurry!" Rudolf warned. "The rain will start any minute."

C-r-a-a-a-a-a-c-c-k-k-k!
The lightning flashed! The thunder roared!
But everyone was safely inside the school bus.

No one got even the tiniest bit wet.
Not even Farmer Fox's tractor.
It was the best rainy-day picnic ever.

At the Air Fair

There is a fair at the airport.
Everyone has come to see, or take rides in, the old
fashioned aeroplanes. All these old aeroplanes have
propellers to help them fly through the air.

Attention, all pilots!
Please do not bump into any runaway balloons.

There is a new jet aeroplane at the fair, too.
Jet planes don't need propellers to make them fly.

Look at Benny Baboon. He is going to show you
something with a toy balloon.

First, he blows up the balloon with air.
But he does not tie a knot in it.
Instead, he lets go of the balloon.
The air begins to rush out of the hole at
the end. As the air rushes out, it pushes
the balloon away from Benny.

control tower

weatherman

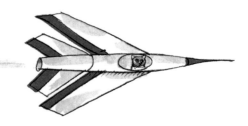

The air is going…

going…

gone!

Rudolf's jet plane engine works a little like a balloon.
Up front, air is sucked into the engine.

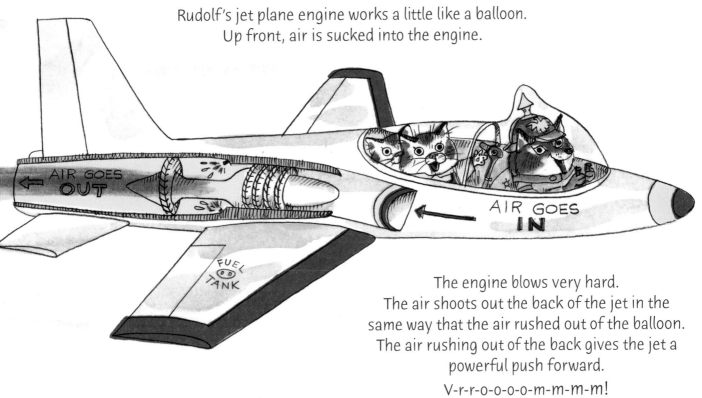

AIR GOES OUT

AIR GOES IN

FUEL TANK

The engine blows very hard.
The air shoots out the back of the jet in the
same way that the air rushed out of the balloon.
The air rushing out of the back gives the jet a
powerful push forward.
V-r-r-o-o-o-o-m-m-m-m!

A Trip by Plane

The Cat family was going to visit Grandma on her birthday.
They rode in a taxi to the small country airport nearby.

There they climbed into a helicopter
to go to the big city airport.

On the way, they saw Sergeant Murphy down below.
He was unscrambling a big traffic jam. Everyone seemed
to be heading towards the airport.

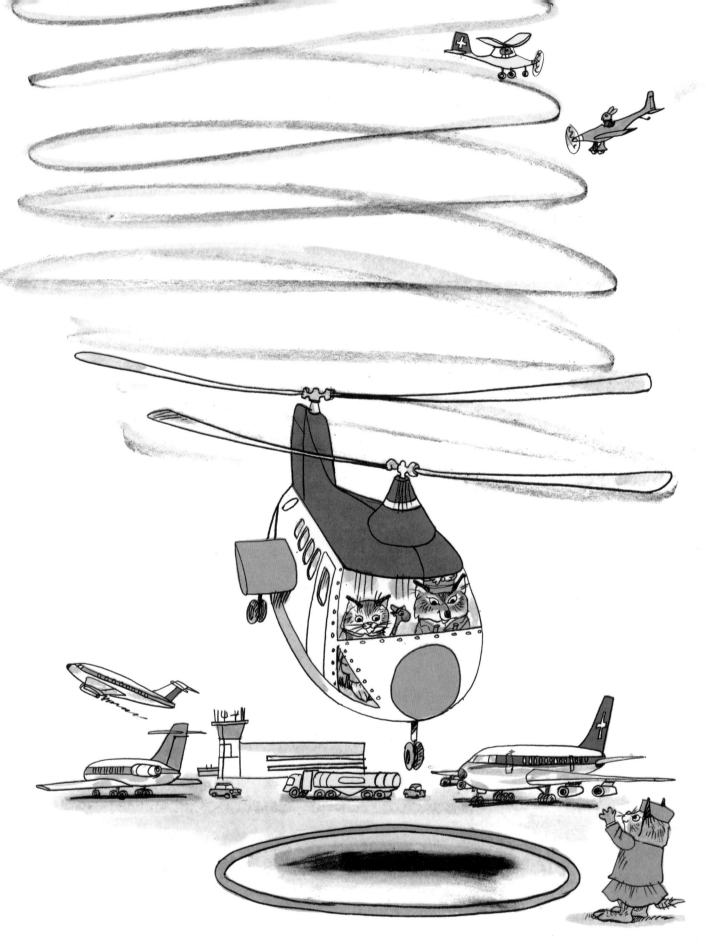

At the city airport, the whirling blades gently lowered the helicopter to the ground.
For the rest of the journey the Cat family would be travelling by jet airliner.

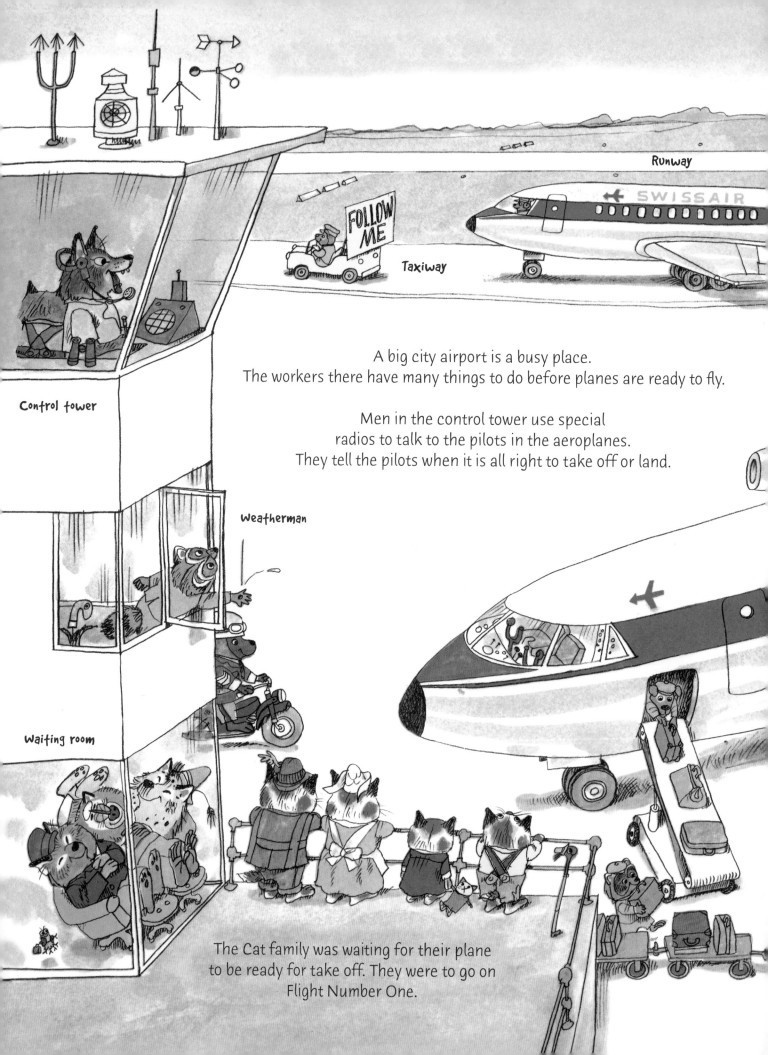

Runway

SWISSAIR

Taxiway

FOLLOW ME

Control tower

A big city airport is a busy place.
The workers there have many things to do before planes are ready to fly.

Men in the control tower use special
radios to talk to the pilots in the aeroplanes.
They tell the pilots when it is all right to take off or land.

Weatherman

Waiting room

The Cat family was waiting for their plane
to be ready for take off. They were to go on
Flight Number One.

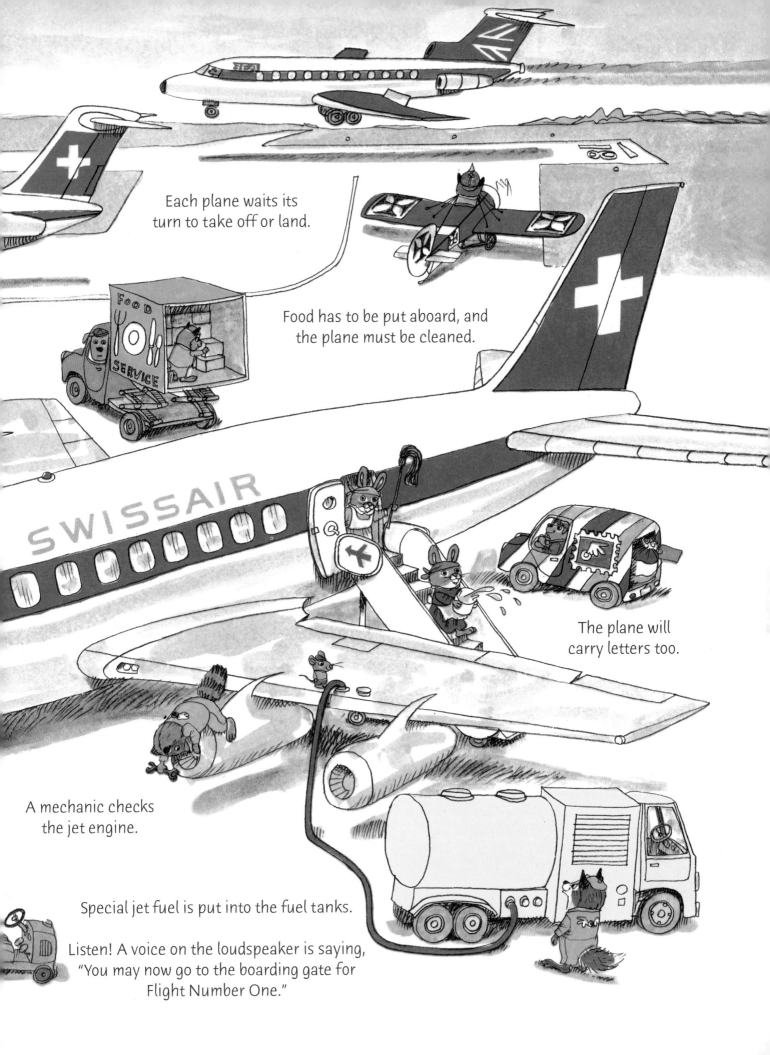

Each plane waits its turn to take off or land.

Food has to be put aboard, and the plane must be cleaned.

The plane will carry letters too.

A mechanic checks the jet engine.

Special jet fuel is put into the fuel tanks.

Listen! A voice on the loudspeaker is saying, "You may now go to the boarding gate for Flight Number One."

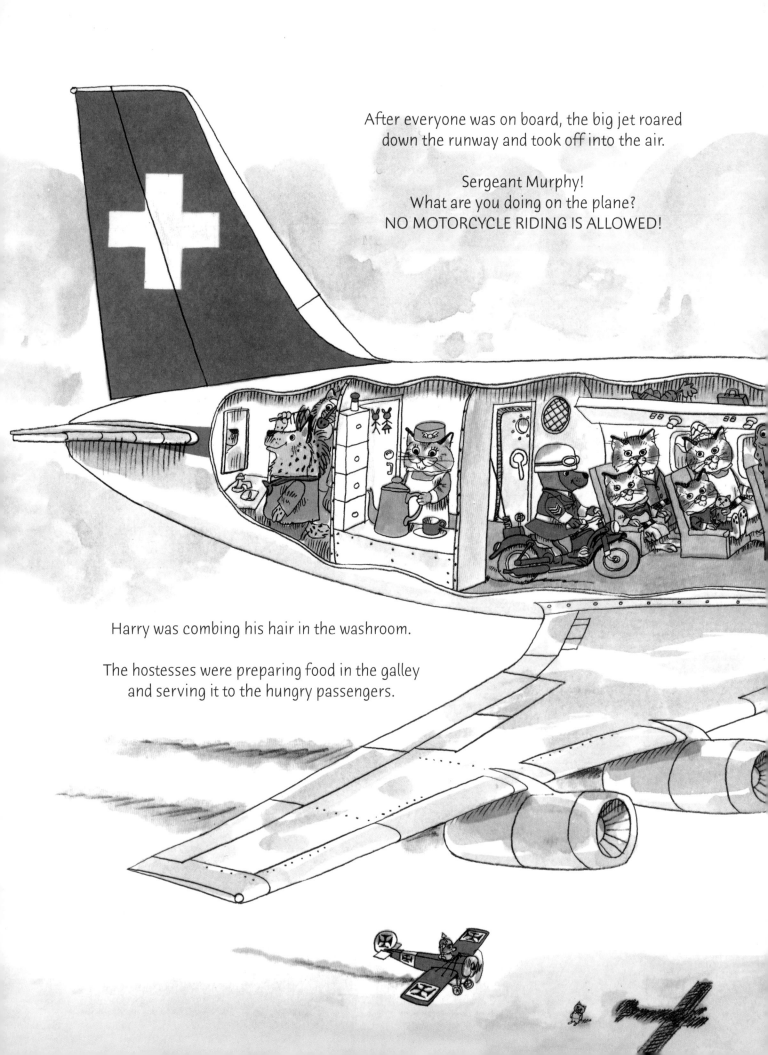

After everyone was on board, the big jet roared
down the runway and took off into the air.

Sergeant Murphy!
What are you doing on the plane?
NO MOTORCYCLE RIDING IS ALLOWED!

Harry was combing his hair in the washroom.

The hostesses were preparing food in the galley
and serving it to the hungry passengers.

Every plane flies in the air lane assigned to it.
In that way, planes don't bump into each other.

Captain Fox is flying the plane with the help of his co-pilot.
The navigator is planning the plane's route in the sky.

NAVIGATOR

"Attention, please!
This is your captain speaking.
Everybody fasten your seatbelt.
We are about to land."

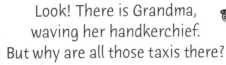

Look! There is Grandma,
waving her handkerchief.
But why are all those taxis there?

The Cat family's plane landed, and Lowly gave Grandma a big kiss.
A lot of other planes landed, too.
Everyone was coming to Grandma's birthday party.
That was why Grandma brought along so many taxis.
They were going to take all her friends to her house.

Sergeant Murphy had come along just to unscramble the big taxi jam!
A good thing, too, or no one would ever get to the party.

"Why, Rudolf!" shouted Sergeant Murphy.
"How did you ever get your plane into this taxi jam?"

Air is very important for blowing
out birthday candles.
Grandma's cake had so many candles
she couldn't blow them out all by herself,
so all her friends helped her.
W-H-O-O-O-O-S-H!
Happy Birthday, Grandma!

Grandma had such a good time at her party that
she can hardly wait until next year.

A Trip to the Moon

Wolfgang Wolf, Benny Baboon and Harry Hyena
are about to climb aboard their spacecraft.
They are going to the moon to collect rock
samples and bring them back to earth.
They want to find out what the moon is made of.

Ready for lift-off.
Five, four, three, two, one, LIFT-OFF!
Up, up goes the spaceship – off into
space and heading for the moon.

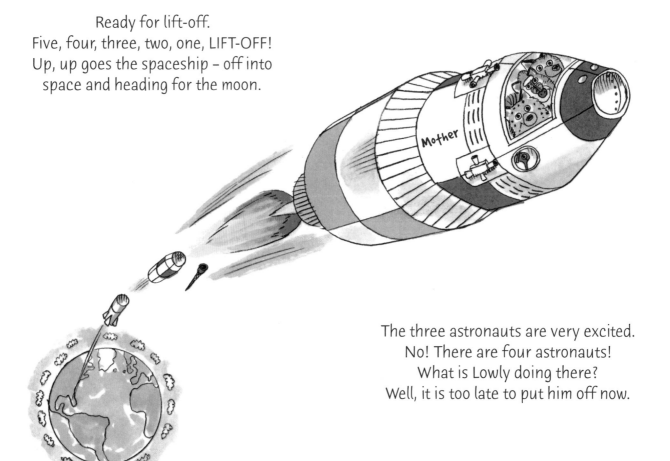

The three astronauts are very excited.
No! There are four astronauts!
What is Lowly doing there?
Well, it is too late to put him off now.

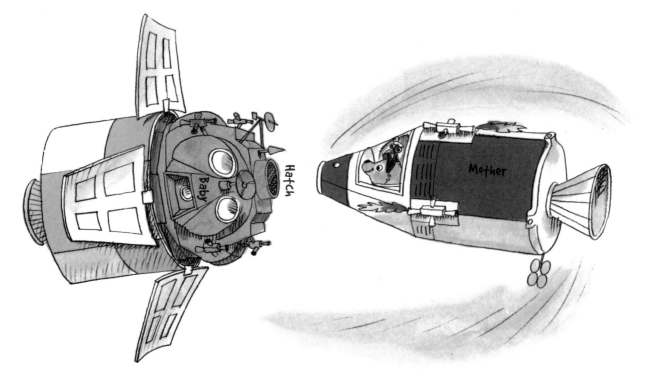

The spacecraft is getting close to the moon.
The landing ship (Baby) is attached to the command ship (Mother).
Wolfgang turns the nose of the command ship around so that it fits
into the hatch door of the landing ship.

Then Benny, Harry and Lowly climb through
the hatch door into the landing ship.
Wolfgang stays behind in the command ship to
wait for their return.
The two ships separate so that the landing
ship can head for the moon.

Benny! Turn on your landing motor so you can
make a gentle landing on the moon.

The ship trips over a rock.
It does not land very gently.

There is no air on the moon.
Each astronaut has to carry his air
with him. It is carried in a tank in the
pack on the astronaut's back.
But Lowly has no space suit so
he gets into Harry's suit.
Now he too can breathe air.
Pick, pick, pick.
They are busy collecting rock samples.

It is time to climb back into the landing ship.
The air in the astronauts' tanks is almost all used up.
Inside the landing ship there is plenty of air for breathing.

Oh, dear!
The hatch door won't
stay closed!

The air inside the landing ship will leak out.
"Keep calm," says Lowly. "Benny, you hold the door shut. Harry, you turn
on the air tank. Then I will be able to breathe when I get out of your spacesuit.
I know how to keep the hatch door closed."

Lowly ties himself into a knot around the door
handle, and the door stays tightly shut.
"Now we will be able to get back with our
valuable rocks," says Lowly.

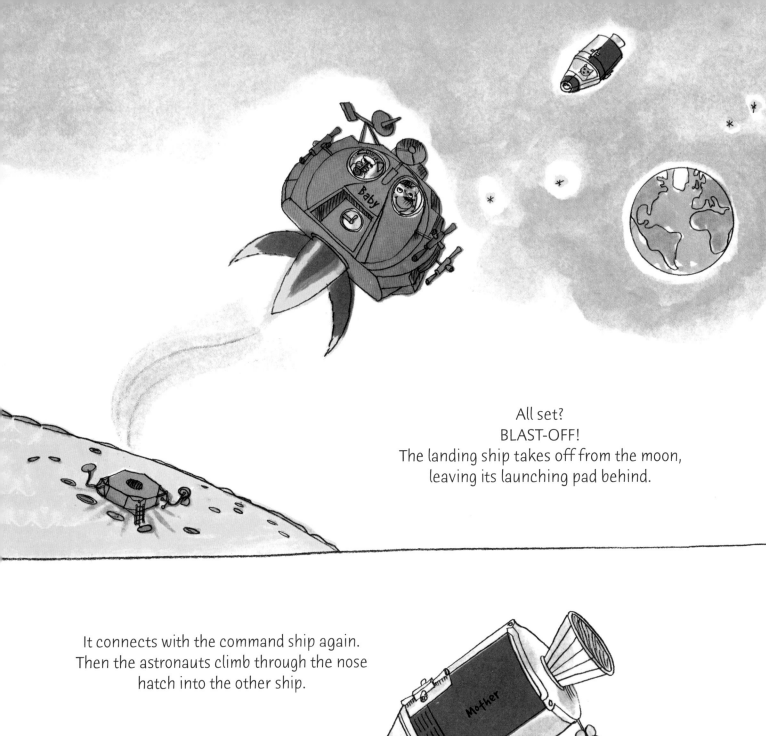

All set?
BLAST-OFF!
The landing ship takes off from the moon,
leaving its launching pad behind.

It connects with the command ship again.
Then the astronauts climb through the nose
hatch into the other ship.

As soon as they are all
set, Wolfgang sends
the empty landing craft
into space. Then
the command ship
heads back to earth.

After the astronauts get back into the earth's atmosphere,
they open up the big parachutes on their spaceship.
An aircraft carrier and several helicopters are waiting to pick them up out of the sea.
HERE THEY COME!...

But the spaceship does not land in the water.
It goes… RIGHT DOWN THE FUNNEL!
Well anyway, the astronauts have landed safely
with their precious rocks.

Everyone is happy to see the brave astronauts safely back on earth.

After they have all had a bath, the admiral
gives Lowly a shiny medal.
On the medal are the words:

"Lowly Worm, a real astro-knot.
The first worm on the moon."

Lowly likes his medal very much,
but best of all he likes being back on earth
where he can breathe fresh air again!
All right, everyone! Let's all take a deep breath
of the earth's wonderful air!

Hay baler

Tractor driver

Cabbage picker

Grass mower

Farm hand

Fence builder

Poster-paster

Woodcutter

Hay lifter

wall builder

Grandma Cat Comes to Visit

Grandma Cat is coming to visit the Cat family. The
whole family drives to the airport to meet her.
As the car passes Farmer Goat's farm, Lowly asks,
"Can we stop and buy some apples?"
Father Cat says, "No. We don't want to be late
arriving at the airport."

Surveyor

Windmill
fixer

Apple picker

Lightning rod
installer

TV

Apple gatherer

Apple-sauce cooker

Corn picker

APPLES

Apple seller

Water pumper

Pumpkin seller

Apple eater

Glider pilot

Helicopter pilot

Air-traffic controller

They arrive at the airport ahead of time. While they wait for Grandma's plane to come in, Lowly visits the flight compartment of a plane that will soon take off. He would like to be an aeroplane pilot. Huckle visits the airport control tower. He would like to be an air-traffic controller and tell the planes when to land and take off. What would YOU like to do at an airport?

Radar controller

Ground controller

Weatherman

TV

Pilot

LOUNGE

Co-pilot

flight engineer

Pilot

flight attendant

BUSYTOWN AIRPORT

TO ALL FLIGHTS

CHECK-IN COUNTER

TAXI

Mr. frumble, the upside-down pilot

Parachutist

Balloonist

FOLLOW ME

Aeroplane washer

SWISSAIR

Stewardess

fuel man

FUEL

Postman

AIRMAIL POST OFFICE

Luggage porter

Here comes Grandma's plane now. But why is she travelling on a big cargo plane? Why isn't she on a passenger plane?

Mr. Frumble!
You're washing
the wrong plane!

food-delivery
person

Well! It seems that Grandma was bringing so many apples with her that she had to come on a cargo plane. Grandma plans to make lots of apple pies on her visit.
"Hi, Grandma. It's good to see you," says Huckle.
"And all your apples, too!" says Lowly.

Katie Morag
and the Wedding

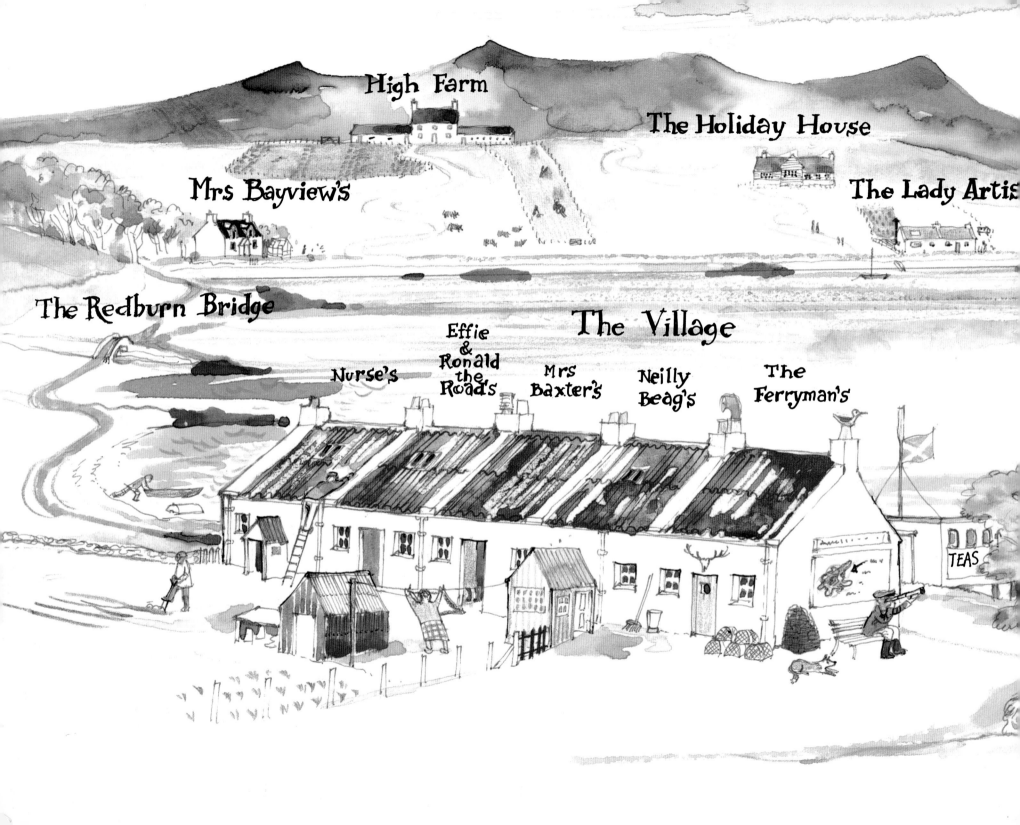

High Farm

The Holiday House

Mrs Bayview's

The Lady Artist's

The Redburn Bridge

The Village

Nurse's

Effie & Ronald the Road's

Mrs Baxter's

Neilly Beag's

The Ferryman's

TEAS

Grannie's

The Mainland

The New Pier

The Jetty

ISLE of STRUAY
SHOP & POST OFFICE

OBAN TIMES
GET YOUR COPY HERE

BISTRO

TO THE NEW PIER

CRAFTS

WELCOME

WEST HIGHLAND FREE PRESS

ORDER NOW

LITTER

The Shop & Post Office

For the Flautist

KATIE MORAG AND THE WEDDING
A RED FOX BOOK 978 1 862 30939 5

First published in Great Britain by The Bodley Head,
an imprint of Random House Children's Books
A Random House Group Company

Bodley Head edition published 1995
Red Fox edition published 1997
This Red Fox edition published 2010

1 3 5 7 9 8 6 4 2

Red Fox Books are published by Random House Children's Books,
61-63 Uxbridge Road, London W5 5SA

www.**kidsatrandomhouse**.co.uk
www.**rbooks**.co.uk

Addresses for companies within The Random House Group Limited can be found at:
www.**randomhouse**.co.uk/offices.htm

THE RANDOM HOUSE GROUP Limited Reg. No. 954009

A CIP catalogue record for this book is available from the British Library.

Printed in China

Katie Morag
and the Wedding

Mairi Hedderwick

WEDDING INVITATION
The Pleasure of the Company of
The McColls
is requested

RED FOX

Ever since the new pier had been built on the Isle of Struay, Granma Mainland visited regularly.

Katie Morag McColl was delighted to see more of her other grandmother. But most delighted of all the islanders was Neilly Beag. He fancied Granma Mainland and always looked so sad when she went away. Then he would write lots of long letters to her in the city on the mainland and wait impatiently for the mailboat to bring back a reply.

This kept Mrs McColl, the Postmistress, very busy. Everyone on the island said a romance was afoot.

"Maybe even a wedding!" whispered the Ferryman's wife in between serving teas to the visitors.

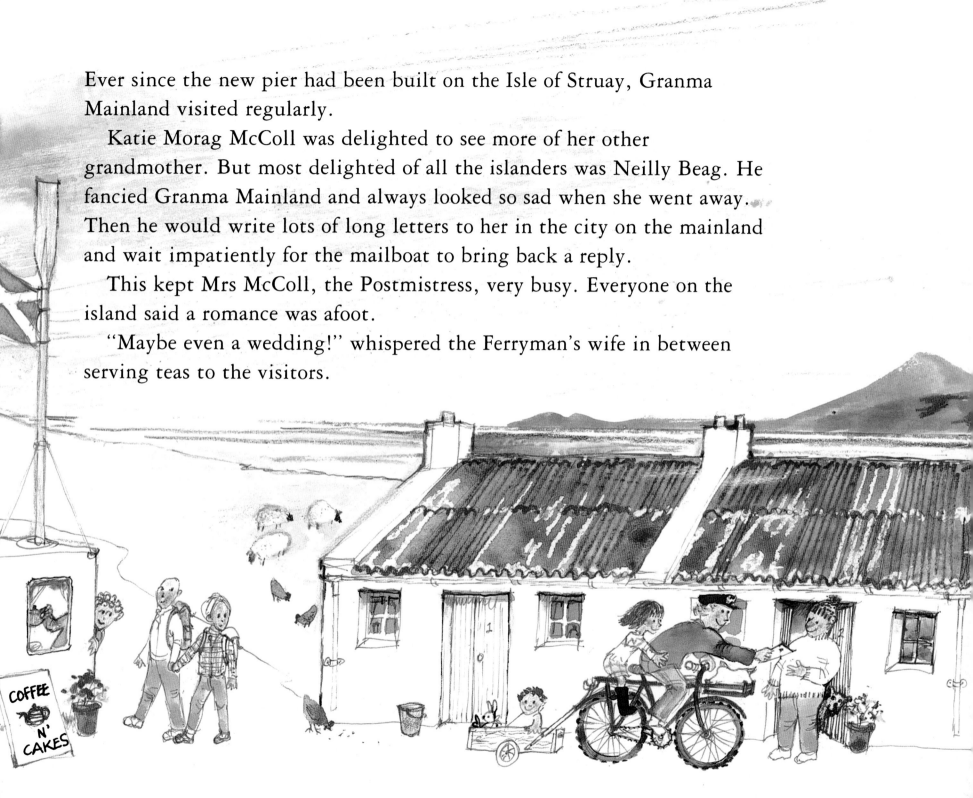

"Pah! A wedding? I'll believe it when I see it!" muttered Grannie Island when she heard the gossip.

Katie Morag was very excited at the thought of a wedding. It usually meant a big party; it also meant that the two people getting married wanted to live together instead of far apart.

Would Granma Mainland come to live in Neilly Beag's house on the island? That would be lovely! But, oh dear, what if Neilly went to live with Granma Mainland in the far away city?

"If there is a wedding will Neilly Beag be our Grandad?" Katie Morag asked when she and Liam arrived at Grannie Island's, just in time for dinner.

Her Grannie did not answer.

"Wheesht! Go sit at the table!" she frowned instead.

"We've got two grandmothers. Why don't we have two grandfathers?"

"Wheesht! Will you SIT DOWN!" glared Grannie Island.

It was a long time since Katie Morag had seen such a glower in Grannie Island's eye. It was time to stop asking questions.

OLD PHOTOS

As Katie Morag pushed Liam homewards she wondered why Grannie Island was in such a bad mood. It made her feel sad.

When they got to the village Neilly Beag was at his front door. He had a huge pile of stamped addressed envelopes in his arms.

"The invitations for the wedding!" he beamed proudly. "Can you take them to the Post Office, Katie Morag?"

That cheered Katie Morag up no end.

"Can *we* go? Can *we* go?" chorused Katie Morag and Liam when the silver and gold invitation was put on the mantelpiece.

"Of course!" smiled Mr and Mrs McColl. "*Everyone* will be going to the wedding!"

"And the new baby?"

"Of course . . ."

"And the Ferryman and his wife . . . and the Lady Artist . . . and the new teacher?"

"Of course! Of course!" laughed Mr and Mrs McColl.

"And Grannie Island?" asked Katie Morag.

Suddenly everything went very quiet in the McColl kitchen. Grown ups can be very strange thought Katie Morag, sometimes they answer questions and sometimes they do not . . .

That night in bed Katie Morag complained to Liam.
"If we didn't answer when we were asked questions we would be called rude."
"Rood!" agreed Liam.

"Granma Mainland always answers questions. I am going to write her a letter," declared Katie Morag.

This is what the letter said:

Me

THE SHOP AND POST OFFICE
ISLE OF STRUAY
Proprietors:
Jean and Peter Nicol McColl

May 27

Dear Granma Manelan,
we are looking fowad to yur
wedding. me ← Liam

Grannie Eyelan is verry
cross. Can you find her a
Gandad too plese ?

lots of luv and XXXXXx
Katie Morag

PS Liam hops you and Neilly hav
lots of babbies

Peedie Peebles
COLOUR
BOOK

The next few weeks on the island were very busy.

All sorts of parcels and crates came off the boat and were carried up to Neilly's house or to the Village Hall.

Neilly dieted so much Mrs McColl had to get a needle and thread to alter his smart new suit. The Ferryman's wife made a giant of a chocolate cake; she and Mr McColl had to stand on stools to decorate it.

Katie Morag and Liam made a special present for the bride and groom. The new baby lent ribbons for flags. Liam thought it was Christmas. He kept chanting "Anta Claws! Anta Claws!" and even hung up his stocking. Katie Morag waited for a reply from Granma Mainland.

The day of the wedding drew near.

Granma Mainland and all the relatives and friends were due to arrive on the boat the day before the big event.

Nobody had seen Grannie Island for days.

I'VE FOUND HIM!

All the islanders went to the pier to meet the guests arriving off the boat, but there was *no* sign of Granma Mainland. Neilly Beag was just about to burst into tears when a loud clattering and whirring reverberated around Village Bay.

It was a helicopter and Granma Mainland was right in the front with the white bearded pilot.

"Anta Claws!" yelled Liam.

"It isn't Santa Claus, silly!" cried Katie Morag. *She* knew who it was.

Grandad Island swung Katie Morag up in the air. "Last time I saw you, Katie Morag, you were just a sparkle in your mum and dad's eyes!"

Katie Morag and Liam raced Grandad Island up to the Village Hall to help with the decorations for the wedding party.

Grandad Island asked if Grannie Island was going to the wedding.

"You'd better go and find out for yourself," said Granma Mainland, somewhat sternly.

Katie Morag watched Grandad Island set off on the long walk round to Grannie Island's house, on the other side of the bay. She worried that the fierce glare in Grannie Island's eye of late would frighten him away.

The Wedding Menu

BSTER CLAW SOUP
OR
TUFFED TURNIP
~
GGIS BURGERS
OR
RROT STEAKS
~
CHIPS
~
AKE & ICECREAM

Katie Morag need not have worried.

On the day of the wedding nobody's eyes were glaring – everyone's eyes were sparkling, especially the two grandads'. But Grannie Island's and Granma Mainland's were the brightest and sparkliest eyes of all.

Granma Mainland and Neilly Beag were to honeymoon on the neighbouring island of Fuay. There were no people on Fuay, only sheep, and they all belonged to Neilly.

"And all the lambs next spring will be yours, Mrs Beag, my wee Bobby Dazzler!"

Liam was right. Granma Mainland *was* going to have lots of babies to look after.

GOOD LUCK

Sheep Dip

JUST MARRIED

But Granma Mainland was not going to give up her flat in the city. She and Neilly would commute between Struay, Fuay and the mainland. And Katie Morag could visit whenever she wanted.

It took a lot of persuading to get Grannie Island up in the helicopter.
Grannie Island did not like travelling.

Grandad Island loved travelling and never stayed in one place for long.

"East, West, Home's Best!" insisted Grannie Island, clinging to her seat like a limpet.

Katie Morag knew then, that Grandad Island would be leaving soon.

"Grandad, when you go travelling can I come too sometimes?"

"Certainly, Katie Morag – anywhere in the world."

Katie Morag was thrilled. She looked forward to visiting Fuay, the city on the mainland and now, anywhere in the world!

But it was good to know that Grannie Island would always be there on the Island of Struay when she got back home.

Join Katie Morag on more adventures!